A Sesame Street Start-to-Read Book™

NOBODY

**Featuring
Jim Henson's
Sesame Street Muppets**

Library of Congress Cataloging in Publication Data:
Roberts, Sarah. Nobody cares about me! (A Sesame Street start-to-read book). SUMMARY: Being sick is not as much fun as Big Bird imagined even though his friends come to visit. [1. Sick—Fiction. 2. Friendship—Fiction] I. Henson, Jim. II. Mathieu, Joe, ill. III. Sesame Street. IV. Children's Television Workshop. V. Title. VI. Series: Sesame Street start-to-read books. PZ7.R54428No [E] AACR2 81–15913
ISBN: 0–394–85177–3 (trade); 0–394–95177–8 (lib. bdg.)

Manufactured in the United States of America   13 14 15 16 17 18 19 20

CARES ABOUT ME!

by Sarah Roberts

illustrated by Joe Mathieu

Random House/
Children's Television Workshop

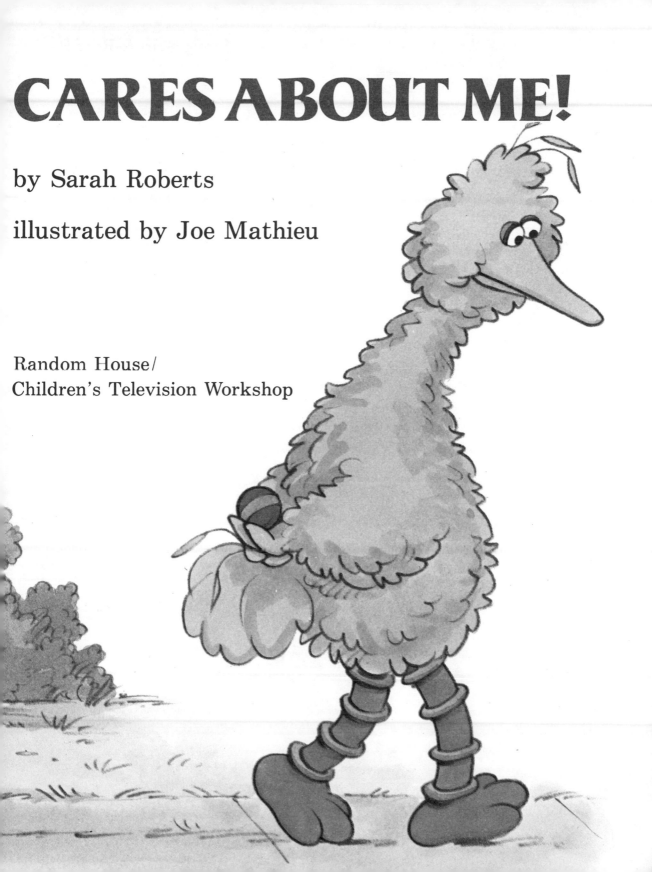

Big Bird was looking
for someone to play with.
"Here comes Bert,"
said Big Bird. "I bet he
will play catch with me."

"Hi, Bert!" said Big Bird.
"Let's play catch."

Bert kept on walking.

"Not today," said Bert.

"Ernie is waiting for me."

Big Bird looked surprised.

"Oh," he said.

Just then Grover ran
out of his house.

He had a shiny new truck.
"Hi, Grover!" said Big Bird.
"That's a nice truck.
  Let's play with it."
  Grover kept on running.
"I am sorry, Big Bird,
  but I am giving it to Ernie,"
  said Grover.
  Big Bird looked sad.
"Oh," he said.

Then Big Bird saw Cookie Monster.
He had a big box of cookies.
"Hi, Cookie! Want to play?"
Cookie shook his head.
"Me bring Ernie cookies,"
said Cookie.

Big Bird looked mad.

"Nuts!" he said.

"No nuts!" said Cookie Monster.

"Cookies!"

Big Bird sat on the steps.

He felt terrible.

"Nobody cares about me!" he cried.

"Just Ernie, Ernie, Ernie!"

Just then Betty Lou came by.

"Why are you so mad?"
she asked Big Bird.

"Nobody will play with me.
Everybody wants to play
with Ernie," he said.

"Oh, Big Bird, didn't you know?
Ernie is sick!" said Betty Lou.
Big Bird looked surprised.
"Oh!" he said. "Well, I am sorry
that Ernie is sick, but I bet
he is having fun."

Betty Lou took Big Bird's hand.
"You are silly. It is not fun
to be sick," she said.
"Come on. Let's visit him."
"Okay," said Big Bird.

Ernie was in bed.
Bert was trying
to feed Ernie some soup.

"How do you feel?"
   asked Big Bird.
"Terrible," said Ernie.
"I have a bad . . . a-A-ACHOO!"
"You have a bad cold,"
   said Betty Lou.
"I know," said Ernie.
   He blew his nose.

"Gee, Ernie," said Big Bird.
"Bert made you some good soup.
Grover gave you a new truck.
Even Cookie was nice to you.
You are so lucky to be sick."
Ernie blew his nose again.

"Lucky?" said Ernie.
"I feel AWFUL!
I feel too sick to eat
and too sick to play.
Being sick is no fun!"

But Big Bird was not so sure.
Later that day he sat in his nest
and said to himself,
"Everybody cares about you
when you are sick."
And then he got an idea.
"I will PRETEND to be sick!"

Just then Little Bird came by
to visit his friend.
"Oh, I am SO sick!"
said Big Bird.
"That is too bad,"
said Little Bird.
"I will make you feel better."

Big Bird smiled.

And Little Bird got busy.

He filled a hot-water bottle.

He swept out Big Bird's nest.

He told Big Bird a bedtime story.

Then he said, "Go to sleep.

I will stay with you."

Big Bird sighed happily.

The next morning Ernie
came to Big Bird's nest.
"Wake up, Big Bird!" he called.
"I am all better. Want to play?"
Big Bird slowly opened his eyes.
"I am sorry, Ernie," said Little Bird.
"But Big Bird can't go out today.
He is sick."

Big Bird jumped out of his nest.
"I am not sick!" he said.

"But you were SO sick
    last night," said Little Bird.
"Well, I am not . . . a-A-ACHOO! . . .
    sick now," sneezed Big Bird.

"You sound sick. How do you feel?"
asked Ernie.
"Sort of hot and cold and funny
in the tummy," said Big Bird.
"Get into your nest," said Ernie.
"I will get Doctor Getwell."

Soon Big Bird felt really sick.

He was glad to see Doctor Getwell.

The doctor felt Big Bird's tummy.

He listened to Big Bird's heart.

He looked in Big Bird's mouth.
"You have a cold," he said.
"I know," said Big Bird.
The doctor told him to drink lots
of juice and get lots of rest.
"Get well," said Doctor Getwell.

Lots of Big Bird's friends
came to visit him.
Bert made him a bowl of soup.
Grover gave him a Yo-Yo.
Cookie gave him cookies.

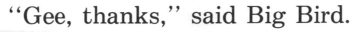

"Gee, thanks," said Big Bird.
"But I feel too sick to eat
and too sick to play."

Big Bird slept a lot that day.
That night he said to Little Bird,
"Ernie was right.
Being sick is no fun.
I feel terrible."
Big Bird sneezed.
"You will feel better soon,"
said Little Bird.

And Little Bird was right.
In a few days Big Bird felt fine.
He ran to the park.
"I am all better! Isn't that great?"
he said to his friends.
"It sure is, because it is no fun
to be sick," they said.

"Boy, you can say that again!"
said Big Bird.
And they all said it again!